THE
MAGIC STOVE

by Mirra Ginsburg

illustrated by Linda Heller

Coward-McCann, Inc.   New York

Text copyright © 1983 by Mirra Ginsburg
Illustrations copyright © 1983 by Linda Heller
All rights reserved. This book, or parts thereof, may
not be reproduced in any form without permission in
writing from the publishers. Published simultaneously
in Canada by General Publishing Co. Limited, Toronto.
Designed by Nanette Stevenson
First printing
Printed in the United States of America

Library of Congress Cataloging in Publication Data
Ginsburg, Mirra.   The magic stove.
Summary: An old man, his wife, and their
rooster enjoy the delicious pies their magic stove
bakes for them, until a greedy king comes to visit.
[1. Folklore—Soviet Union.   2. Roosters—Fiction.
3. Stoves—Fiction] I. Heller, Linda, ill. II. Title.
PZ8.1.G455Mag   1983   398.2'1'0947 [E] 82-12523
ISBN 0-698-20566-9

To Osik and Becky
MG

For my mother
LH

Once upon a time there lived an old man and his wife. They were very, very poor. They had no cow, and no horse, no pigs, and no geese. All they had was a rooster, with a bright red comb and a fine curved tail. And the three of them lived in a tiny hut.

One morning the old man said to the old woman:
"Let us have some breakfast. I am hungry."
But the old woman said:
"Oh, my good husband, we have no food left in the house. I am hungry too."
She looked in the cupboards and on the shelves, and all she found was a small dry crust.
"Well," said the old man. "That's fine too."

He broke the crust in half, brought a glass of water, and put the pieces in to soak, to soften them. Suddenly he heard:

"Ko-ko, ko-ko!"

It was the rooster, with the bright red comb and the fine curved tail. He was hungry too.

The old man shared his piece with the rooster. Then he thought, let me look in the garden. Perhaps I'll find a potato or a carrot that we missed under some bush.

He went out, and the rooster went out behind him. The
old man looked here, and he looked there, but could not
find anything at all.

Meantime the rooster was not idle, either. He was busy digging a hole, scratching the earth with his claws, sweeping it away with his wings, and crying:

"Ko-ko-ko! Ko-ko-ko!"

The old man came over and looked down. Something
was glowing brightly in the hole. It was a little iron stove.
The old man picked it up, and put it down on a stump,
and said:

"Wouldn't it be nice if the stove baked us a pie, with
eggs and scallions in it?"

The rooster tapped the stove with his beak:

"Ko-ko!"

"What can this mean?" the old man asked.

He opened the door of the stove, and— Oh-h! What a
pie! Crisp and brown, and fluffy, and filled with eggs and

scallions. The old man snatched the pie and took a great big bite. Then another. And another. And the pie was gone.

"Oh," he cried. "What have I done? The old woman at home is hungry too. We've always shared and shared alike. And now I ate the whole pie by myself."

But the rooster with the bright red comb and the fine curved tail pecked at the stove again.

The old man opened the stove door. And there was another pie in it, even better than the first. He picked up the little stove and ran home.

"How would you like a pie, old woman?" he said. "With anything you wish in it?"

"Stop teasing," his wife cried angrily. "I'd be glad to have a piece of bread, and you talk of pies."

The old man opened the stove and gave her the pie. She ate it, and asked for another, with cheese and apples. The stove baked another pie, with cheese and apples.

From that day on they had enough to eat. The stove baked for them any kind of pie they asked. Even the rooster got whatever he wanted. And the three of them began to live like kings.

One evening the old woman sat by the window, spinning and singing, when the king himself rode by. She ran out to welcome him.

"Give me a drink of water, old woman," he asked. "I've been riding all day, and I am tired and thirsty."

"Come in, come in," she said. "And how would you like a bite to eat?"

"Fine," said the king. "What do you have for me?"

"A pie," said the old woman. "Our little magic stove will give you any kind you choose."

"Well," said the king. "Then how about a pie with fresh wild strawberries?"

It was late autumn, and the wild strawberries were long gone. But the woman opened the little stove, and out came a pie with fresh wild strawberries.

The king ate it and didn't say a word. Then he asked:
"Can you put me up for the night? It is late, and my
palace is a long journey away."

They made a bed for him on the bench near the door.

And they all settled down for the night. The old man on the large brick oven. The rooster beneath the oven. The old woman on a cot. And the king on the bench by the door.

After a while the king said:
"Old man, old man, are you asleep?"
The old man didn't answer. He was fast asleep.
The king said:
"Old woman, old woman, are you asleep?"
The old woman didn't answer. She was fast asleep.
The king picked up the little stove, put it in his pouch,
and hurried out of the hut.

The old man heard nothing. The old woman heard nothing. But the rooster with the bright red comb and the fine curved tail heard and saw everything.

He stole out after the king, jumped up behind him on the horse, and rode with him to the king's palace.

The next day the king invited all the nobles and their wives and sons and daughters to a great feast at the palace.

They came in carriages and on horseback, dressed in their finest clothes. But all they found in the dining hall was an empty table, with nothing on it. Not even bread and salt. Only a little iron stove.

But then the king came out and welcomed them handsomely, and announced with pomp and pride:

"This feast, my dearest guests, will be a very special one. We shall feast on pies. Let everybody name the pie he wants, and he shall have it."

One guest cried:
"I want a pie with kasha!"
Another cried:
"A potato pie!"
Others asked for pies with apples, with cherries, with
meat, with cabbage, with currants, and carrots, and what-
ever else came to their minds.

Suddenly there was a flash of bright feathers, a flapping of wings. What was it? Why, the rooster! He leaped up on the windowsill and cried:

"Cock-a-doodle-do! This king is a thief! A thief! Give the little stove back to my old man!"

The king turned fiery red. Who dared to call him a thief? He stamped his feet. He turned to his servants and cried:

"My faithful servants! Catch this lying rooster and throw him into the deep, deep pond."

The faithful servants came running, caught the rooster with the bright red comb and the fine curved tail, and threw him into the deep, deep pond.

The rooster lay at the bottom of the pond, and he said to himself:

"This isn't the worst thing that could have happened. It could have been much worse. Now, my beak, drink up the water, drink it up, drink it up."

And he drank up the whole deep pond. And again he leaped up on the windowsill.

"Cock-a-doodle-do! This king is a thief. Give the stove back to my old man!"

The king turned purple with rage and cried:

"My faithful servants! Catch this lying rooster and throw him into the oven, right into the fire!"

The faithful servants seized the rooster and threw him into the oven, right into the blazing fire.

And the rooster lay in the blazing fire and said to himself:

"This isn't the worst thing that could have happened. It could have been much worse. Now, my beak, spill out the water, spill it out, spill it out."

And he spilled the whole deep pond into the oven. The fire went out, and the water poured out of the oven and onto the floor, higher and higher, until all the guests and the king stood up to their ankles, up to their knees in water. And still the water rose and rose, and the rooster flew up on the windowsill and kept crying:

"Cock-a-doodle-do! This king is a thief! Give the stove back to my old man, give it back!"

The guests threw down their pies and ran out of the palace hall as fast as they could, with wet feet and dripping clothes. They got into their carriages and on their horses and galloped away. But the king was greedy and would not return the little magic stove. He ran with it around and around the table. The rooster flew up on his head and pecked and pecked, crying:

"Give it back, give it back!"

And the water kept rising and rising.

At last the king could not endure it any longer. He threw the little stove on the table and ran toward the door. But he slipped on a pie and—Plop!—stretched out in the water.

And the rooster with the bright red comb and the fine curved tail caught the little stove under his wing. "Ko-ko-ko!" he sang, and he leaped up on the windowsill, leaped down on the ground, and hurried back to the old man and the old woman.

And there they are to this day, eating pies, and singing songs, and never troubled any more by thieving kings.